Tiger Woods

YOUNG CHAMPION

Tiger Woods

YOUNG CHAMPION

by Joanne Mattern
illustrated by Robert F. Goetzl

Tiger Woods

YOUNG CHAMPION

Fifteen thousand people lined the thirty-fifth hole of the Witch Hollow Golf Course near Portland, Oregon, to watch the finals of the U.S. Amateur championship. Despite the crowd, there was total silence. Everyone was focused on one golfer: an eighteen-year-old named Tiger Woods.

Just a little while earlier, Tiger had been losing. Halfway through the thirty-six-hole match, he was five strokes behind a young golfer named Steve Scott. But Tiger always seemed to play best under a lot of pressure. As the afternoon wore on, he hit one amazing shot after another. Steve Scott watched his lead grow smaller and smaller. Now, with only two holes left to play, Woods had a chance to tie the match.

Despite the pressure, the young man was perfectly calm. He looked at the hole, thirty feet away. He pictured in his mind exactly where he wanted the ball to go. Then he took three practice strokes, paused, and looked at the hole again. Finally, Tiger swung his club. The ball rolled across the green and dropped directly into the hole, as the crowd screamed with excitement.

Tiger Woods went on to win the match and the 1994 U.S. Amateur championship. It was a historic day, for not only was Tiger Woods the first African-American to win the title, he was also the youngest player ever to achieve this victory! But for Tiger, it was only one more victory in a golf career that had started when he was just a baby.

Eldrick Woods was born on December 30, 1975. He is the only child of Earl Woods, an African-American retired army officer, and his wife, Kultida, who is originally from Thailand. Kultida chose the name Eldrick, creating it by combining some of the letters from her first name and Earl's. But from the day his son was born, Earl called him "Tiger," in honor of a close friend who had saved his life during the Vietnam War.

Tiger grew up in a small house in Cypress, California. Earl Woods had learned to play golf only shortly before Tiger was born. The boy's father loved the game so much that he set up a piece of carpet and a net in the garage so he could practice his shots.

Every day, Earl would put Tiger's high chair in the garage so the baby could watch his daddy hit ball after ball. Tiger was so fascinated with the game that he cried when his mother came in to feed him. Nothing was more interesting to little Tiger than watching his father play golf.

One day, when Tiger was ten months old, he gave his parents a big surprise. He climbed out of his high chair, picked up a golf club that Earl had cut down to a smaller size for him, and put a ball on the tee. Then he looked at his target, waved his club, and hit the ball right into the net.

"I almost fell off my chair," says Tiger's dad. He raced into the house, calling for Kultida to come and see. "We have a genius on our hands!" he yelled.

Soon the hallway between the living room and one of the bedrooms became Tiger's golf course. He'd chase a tennis ball up and down the hall, hitting it with the hose from the vacuum cleaner. Eventually, Earl decided it was time for Tiger to play on a real course. He took his son to the navy golf course in Los Alamitos when Tiger was still in diapers.

Little Tiger and his father loved to practice together. By the time he was two years old, Tiger had memorized his father's phone number at work. Every afternoon, the boy would call and ask, "Daddy, can I practice with you today?" The answer was always yes.

Around that time, Tiger entered a golf competition for boys ten and under at the navy course—and he won. Soon the local TV stations were coming to see this two-year-old golf sensation.

It didn't take long for Tiger's fame to spread beyond southern California. When he was three years old, he appeared on *The Mike Douglas Show,* a national talk show. Little Tiger hit some balls with veteran actor and comedian Bob Hope. Then, when he was five, Tiger appeared on the TV show *That's Incredible.* He sat in host Fran Tarkenton's lap, hit whiffle balls into the audience, and wasn't bothered one bit by the crowds or the hot lights of the TV studio.

Tiger's father wanted his young son to understand that while being talented at golf was a good thing, it didn't make Tiger better than other people. To underscore his message, Earl pointed to another guest on *That's Incredible*, a ten-year-old weightlifter. "Can you do that?" he asked Tiger as they watched the girl pick up the show's three hosts.

"No," Tiger replied.

"That's right," Earl told him. "There are a lot of special people in the world, and you're just one of them."

Tiger's love of golf continued to grow. He never tired of practicing the sport. He thought playing golf was the most fun in the world. His parents did all they could to encourage him as he worked to improve his golf game. When Tiger was six years old, Earl brought home a set of motivational tapes. They offered advice and inspiration to help achieve goals. Tiger listened to these messages over and over. He wrote what they meant to him on strips of paper and tacked the strips up on the walls of his room. "I believe in me," he told himself. "My strength is great, and my decisions are strong. I do it all with my heart."

Tiger's father knew that talent and ability were only one part of succeeding in golf competitions. Tiger also had to be emotionally tough. To achieve this goal, when Tiger was eleven years old, Earl began a program of "basic training." Sometimes while the boy was concentrating on making a shot, Earl would try to startle him by coughing, jingling his keys, or dropping a bag full of clubs. He'd roll balls in front of his son just as he was about to shoot. He sometimes even called Tiger names. Earl knew that one day Tiger might face such distractions when competing. He wanted his son to be prepared to deal with difficult situations.

During "basic training," Tiger occasionally got angry at his father, but the boy never told him to stop. And he never allowed his father's tricks to spoil his concentration or his game. After two months, Earl knew his son could face any challenge, no matter how tough or unfair, and still come out on top.

As an adult, Tiger wrote about the help his father had given him: "Pop never pushed me to play. Whether I practiced or played was always my idea. He was instrumental in helping me develop the drive to achieve, but his role—as well as my mother's—was one of support and guidance, not interference."

For his part, Earl just wanted Tiger to develop good values and to be a good human being. He shows how highly he thinks of his son when he says, "I'm very proud that Tiger is a better person than he is a golfer."

Earl never punished Tiger for losing a tournament or making mistakes. There was only one thing he would not tolerate— quitting. Once, when the teenage Tiger played in the Orange Bowl Junior Classic in 1992, he was so angry at himself for missing an easy putt that he began to play as if he didn't care. Tiger lost the tournament, and Earl knew his son had given up without even trying. After the game, Tiger's father gave him a serious talking to. "Golf owes you nothing," said Earl. "Never quit! Do you understand me?"

From then on, Tiger realized he would be a great golfer only if he never gave up. Even when he was losing, he had to play as if the championship depended on every shot.

Tiger's mom also helped her son succeed. She expected him to behave politely and respectfully. Unlike some other young players, Tiger did not fling his clubs or throw a tantrum when things didn't go his way. "I will not have a spoiled child," Kultida told him. But she also encouraged Tiger to win. "When you are ahead, don't take it easy," she said, urging him to press for victory. "After the finish, then be a sportsman." Kultida set a good example for her son by cheering for other players just as enthusiastically as she cheered for Tiger.

Tiger's coaches were also an important part of his success. His first coach, Rudy Duran, began teaching him when Tiger was only four years old. Every hole on a golf course is assigned a *par*, which is the average number of shots a player needs to get the ball from the tee to the cup. Because young Tiger was not yet strong enough to hit real par on the golf course, Duran came up with a rating called "Tiger par" for each hole they played. He based the score on Tiger's strength and ability. By setting small, achievable goals, Duran built Tiger's confidence and made sure that golf was fun for the little boy.

Tiger always set high goals for himself. One day, when he was eleven years old, he came home from school and made a chart to pin up on his bedroom wall. The first column listed every major golf tournament. At the top of the second column, Tiger pasted a picture of Jack Nicklaus, whom many consider to be the greatest golfer of all time. Then Tiger listed the age at which Nicklaus won each tournament. Finally, Tiger wrote his name on top of the third column. "I wanted to be the youngest player ever to win the majors," he later told a reporter from *Sports Illustrated*. "Nicklaus was my hero, and I thought it would be great to accomplish all the things he did even earlier than he accomplished them."

28

As Tiger got older, he entered amateur golf tournaments all over the country. He was too young to travel alone, so Earl resigned from his job to accompany his son. Since the family didn't have a lot of money, Earl and Tiger always arrived just before the tournaments started. That way, they wouldn't have to pay for an extra night at a hotel.

One day, Tiger asked his father if they could get to tournaments a day earlier, so he would have a chance to practice. Earl realized that it wasn't fair to expect Tiger to play well on a course he'd never seen before. From that day on, Tiger's father promised, they would do whatever it took for Tiger to be the best. Their money and efforts paid off. By the time he was twelve years old, Tiger had won several junior world tournaments and was undefeated in southern California's junior golf league.

Despite his growing celebrity in the world of golf, Tiger's everyday life was fairly normal. He attended Western High School, where he studied hard and sometimes went to movies and parties. When he played for the school's golf team, Tiger always carried his own clubs. One time, a TV show called *Scholastic Sports America* asked if they could follow Tiger around school with a camera. Tiger said no. He didn't want anyone at Western to think he was special.

But Tiger *was* special. On July 28, 1991, the fifteen-year-old won his first national golf title, the U.S. Junior Amateur championship. He was the youngest person ever to win the title, and only the third African-American. Tiger later became the first person to win three straight U.S. Amateur titles.

U.S. Junior Amateur
Championship 1991

Tiger and his family have always felt that Tiger should give back to the community. To do this, he has often held golf clinics in minority neighborhoods. Tiger feels he owes it to golf and to young people to introduce children to the sport. "I love doing clinics," Tiger once said. "I think that's the biggest impact I've made so far. It doesn't matter whether the kids are white, black, brown, or green. All that matters is that I touch kids the way I can through these clinics, and that they benefit from them. I have this talent. I might as well use it to benefit somebody."

Tiger thinks that children look up to him because he is practically a kid himself. He loves football, basketball, rap music, video games, and fast food, and he treats his young fans with understanding and respect. Once, when he was playing in Scotland, Tiger was confronted with hundreds of children who wanted his autograph. He pulled the smallest boy in the group out of the crowd and told everyone else to line up behind him. "No one gets an autograph until you do," he told the little boy.

Things haven't always been easy for Tiger Woods. Despite his celebrity and talent, he has been the target of racial discrimination, even on the golf course. He was not allowed to play alone on the navy course as a child—a rule that was never enforced against white children. And Tiger has gotten used to receiving what he calls "the look" when he plays. "It makes you uncomfortable, like someone is saying something without saying it," Tiger says.

Tiger's parents taught him the best way to deal with racial discrimination. "When you've been wronged, when you've been angered, you need not say anything," his mother told him. "Let your clubs speak for you." And that's exactly what Tiger has done.

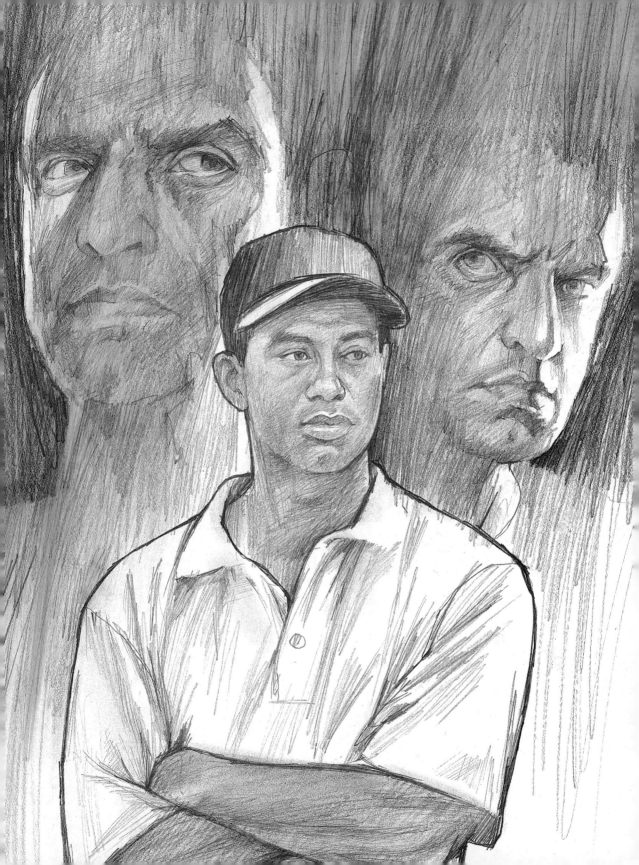

After he graduated from Western High, Tiger entered Stanford University in Palo Alto, California. Stanford is one of the most demanding colleges in the United States, and it was the perfect place for a young man who always put education first. Tiger was happy to find that since there were so many special students at Stanford, no one paid much attention to him. "If it's not the nation's best pianist, or the nation's best swimmer, it's somebody with a brain you can't believe," he said of the Stanford student body. "I'm just lost in a crowd here, which is fine. That's why I came."

Of course, it didn't hurt that Stanford had a terrific golf team. Even when he was a freshman, Tiger was the star of the team. During his summer vacations, he played in many major golf tournaments, including the Masters, the U.S. Open, and the British Open. Although he was still an amateur, Tiger was playing against the biggest names in professional golf—and playing well.

As Tiger finished his second year at Stanford, the sports world buzzed with this intriguing question: When would Tiger leave school to become a professional golfer? Even Tiger wasn't sure what the answer was. School was important to him, but so was golf. He knew he needed to compete against the best players in order for his own game to improve—and he couldn't do that while attending college full-time.

Finally, in August 1996, Tiger Woods answered the question everyone was asking. He promised his parents he would finish school in the future; then he announced he was turning pro.

Tiger Woods
1997

Tiger took the professional golf world by storm. He won two of his first seven tournaments and finished in the top ten in three others. Then, in April 1997, he traveled to Augusta, Georgia, to play in the world-famous Masters Tournament.

The Masters is one of the toughest courses on the golf circuit, but Tiger was up to the challenge. Just twenty-one years old, he blew past the best golfers in the world to become the youngest Masters winner ever. Not only that, but Tiger's score of 270 was 18 under par—the lowest score in tournament history! This was the tournament Tiger had dreamed of winning ever since he was a little boy.

In 1999 and again in 2000, Tiger won the PGA Championship. On July 23, 2000, he won the British Open by eight strokes and became the fifth player in history—and the youngest ever—to complete the career Grand Slam.

The future of Tiger Woods is sure to hold many more triumphs—in golf, as well as in his personal life. He has said he wants to be "the Michael Jordan of golf—the greatest golfer ever." It's a good bet that Tiger will achieve his goal. His dedication to hard work, as well as his love and admiration for his family, his fans, and the game of golf, have put him on top of the world.

Index